Mallory in the Spotlight

For Emma, the actress in our family,
and special thanks to the real
Mrs. Denson for her guidance
—L.B.F.

For my husband Josh, my best friend
—J.K.

Mallory in the Spotlight

by Laurie Friedman

illustrations by Jennifer Kalis

MINNEAPOLIS

CONTENTS

A WORD FROM MALLORY

My name is Mallory McDonald, like the restaurant but no relation, and I have a BIG problem. Actually, I have a B.F.B.B. problem. In case you don't know what that means, I'll tell you. I have a *Best Friend Behaving Badly* problem.

The best friend I'm talking about is Mary Ann, and the reason she's behaving badly is because she's not acting like my best friend. In fact, she's acting like she hardly even knows who I am. I'm not kidding. As far as Mary Ann is concerned, I might as well start wearing a T-shirt that says *I'm Invisible*.

Whenever Mary Ann sees me

6

(which lately, isn't very often), she actually looks the other way and pretends like I'm not even there.

If you're asking yourself why she would do something like that, you can stop asking. I'll tell you the answer in one simple word: JEALOUSY.

That's right. Mary Ann is jealous of me. If you're wondering why she would be jealous of me, I'll tell you that too.

She's jealous because I got something she wants and instead of being happy for me, she's unhappy for herself.

Now do you see what I mean about *Best Friend Behaving Badly*?

Mom says I should talk to Mary Ann. Mom says there are always two sides to every story. But I say this doesn't have anything to do with sides. It has to do with acting. Mary Ann needs to start acting like my best friend.

Period. End of story, which if you ask me, has only one side . . . MINE!

NEWS FLASH

Here's a riddle: Whose name starts with an *A*, her friend's name starts with a *D*, and they're both jumping around my fourth-grade classroom like they're either on a trampoline or really excited about something?

If you guessed Arielle and Danielle, you guessed right.

"News flash!" says Danielle as soon as I walk through the door with my best friends Mary Ann and Joey.

"What's the news?" I ask.

"We know, but we're not telling," says Danielle.

"We got here early so Mr. Knight told us," says Arielle, like the idea that they were here to get the information is almost as exciting as the information itself.

The bell rings. "Class, take your seats, please," says my teacher, Mr. Knight.

"Since you're late, you'll have to wait and hear it when Mr. Knight tells the rest of the class," whispers Arielle.

I give Mary Ann and Joey an *I-know-they're-enjoying-knowing-something-we-don't* look.

"How do you know we even want to know what it is?" I whisper back.

She and Danielle look at each other like they have to hold in their laughter. "Trust me," says Danielle. "You're going to want to know."

Even though I don't like that Arielle and Danielle know something that Mary Ann, Joey, and I don't, I do like that Mr. Knight has something exciting to tell us. I cross my toes. I hope whatever he has to say is as exciting as Arielle and Danielle think it is.

"Class," says Mr. Knight once everyone is seated. "Before we begin our lessons, I have an announcement."

He writes the word *Annie* on the board.

"Fern Falls Elementary is going to be putting on a musical called *Annie*. I am sure some of you are familiar with the plot. If you are not, it is the story of an orphaned girl and her dog and what they go through to find a family."

PLOT
the story, or in simple English, "What it's all about"

Mr. Knight smiles. "It is a heartwarming story, and it will be a lot of fun for everyone at our school who chooses to participate."

A lot of hands go up.

Mr. Knight motions for us to put our hands down. "I'm thrilled to see you're all so enthusiastic. Let me finish explaining, and then you may ask questions.

"The show is open to all students at Fern Falls Elementary. Auditions will be next week. If you are interested in trying out, please come see me. I will give you a preselected piece of the script, which you will need to memorize and recite at the auditions. As *Annie* is a musical, you will also need to be prepared to sing a song of your choice. There will even be some dancing involved for those of you who like to dance."

SCRIPT
the text of a play

Everyone starts talking at the same time. Now I know why Arielle and Danielle were so excited. This is going to be so much fun. "I can't wait to try out," I say to Mary Ann, who is at the desk next to me. "We should pick our songs after school today so we can start practicing."

"OK," says Mary Ann. She picks at the frayed edges of her notebook like that is

much more interesting than picking
a song.

"Aren't you excited to try out?" I ask her.

But before she can answer, Mr. Knight
tells everyone to quiet down. "If anyone
has questions, I'm happy to answer them."

"When is the show?" asks April.

"Next month," says Mr. Knight. "Once
the show is cast, it will take some time for
the actors to memorize their parts and to
get everything ready, like costumes and
scenery."

Joey raises his hand. "What if you don't
want to be in the show, but you want to
help do something else?"

Mr. Knight nods like he approves of the
question. "You will be able to sign up to
be part of the crew," he says. "There will
be all kinds of things for the crew to do like
lighting and scenery and makeup."

Some of the boys laugh. I don't think Joey had makeup in mind when he asked the question.

Pamela Brooks, my good friend and desk mate from last year, raises her hand. "Who is going to be the director of the show?"

DIRECTOR
the person in charge of a show

Mr. Knight smiles again. "That is a surprise. But what I will tell you is that we are bringing in someone very special who has done lots of school plays."

Everyone starts talking at once about the mystery person, but Mr. Knight stops us. "Class, please open your math books and let's continue the section we're doing on fractions."

Mr. Knight starts explaining about dividing a pie into parts. I look at the numerator and denominator he's written on the board. It's hard to think about parts of a pie, even if I imagine that it is my favorite pie, chocolate marshmallow, when all I can think about is *Annie*.

I can't wait to look for a song and start practicing lines from the script.

And I'm not the only one who is thinking about it. At lunch, *Annie* is all that anyone at my table is talking about.

"I can't wait to try out for *Annie*," says Zoe.

"Me too," says Hannah.

"Me three," I say like I haven't been this excited about anything in a long time, and the truth is, I haven't.

Arielle and Danielle look at each other. Then they look at me. "I think it's pretty

obvious that not everyone who tries out
will get a part," says Danielle.

"At least, not a good one," says Arielle.

"We've been dancing for a long time."
Danielle gives Arielle a *we're-going-to-get-
good-parts-because-we're-good-dancers* look.

I know Arielle and Danielle think they
will get great parts and I won't. Usually,
when they say stuff like this, it bothers me.
But today, I'm so excited that I don't let it.

I put my peanut butter and marshmallow sandwich back in my lunch bag. "I'm too excited to eat," I tell Mary Ann. "Want to come over after school, and we can pick our songs?"

"OK," says Mary Ann. But her "*OK*" doesn't sound very enthusiastic.

"C'mon," I say as I drag her out of the cafeteria. "Let's go get the script from Mr. Knight, and we'll have everything we need this afternoon to get started."

"OK," Mary Ann says again like that's what she'll do if I want to, but she doesn't really care if she does it.

I look at my friend. I don't know what part of the script Mr. Knight is going to give us, but for Mary Ann's sake, I hope it has the word *OK* in it.

That's the one word Mary Ann seems to be really good at saying lately.

A TALE OF TWO FRIENDS: PART 1

Once upon a time there were two friends. These friends did everything together. They had sleepovers together. They painted their toenails together. They were even in the same class at school. One day, their teacher announced there was going to be a play at their school.

The first friend (with red hair, bangs,

and lots of freckles), who we will call Girl #1, got super excited. She couldn't wait to try out for the play. The same day that the teacher told them about the play, Girl #1 started getting ready for auditions.

She picked out a song to sing. She started practicing it every chance she got. She brought home the part she was supposed to read at tryouts and rehearsed it in front of the mirror in her bathroom at least three times a day.

Since you already know that the two

friends do everything together, you probably think that the other friend (with curly, blonde hair), who we will call Girl #2, did exactly the same thing. But guess what? That's not what she did.

Girl #2 didn't get excited about the play at all.

She didn't pick out a song to sing. She just said she would sing "whatever." She didn't bring home what she was supposed to read at tryouts. Actually, she did. But then she said she couldn't find it in her backpack. And she didn't even spend any time in front of the mirror in her bathroom.

This worried Girl #1. She tried to explain to her friend how important it was to prepare for the auditions. She told her that if she wanted to get a good part, she would have to work hard on it.

She reminded her that she liked to dance and that she should practice her dancing so she would look good at the audition. She even made up a little rehearsal schedule for her.

MARY ANN'S REHEARSAL SCHEDULE	
MON:	PRACTICE!
TUES:	PRACTICE!
WED:	PRACTICE!
THURS:	PRACTICE!
FRI:	PRACTICE!
SAT:	PRACTICE!
SUN:	PRACTICE!

But nothing she did seemed to make a difference.

It was like Girl #2 either didn't care if she got a good part or thought she would get one whether she was prepared or not.

As the days leading up to tryouts passed, Girl #1 continued to prepare, while Girl #2 didn't. Each day, Girl #1 begged her friend to get her act together. (Act. Actress. Get it?)

But Girl #2 barely seemed to hear what her friend had to say.

As you can imagine, this annoyed Girl #1 because she thought being in a play sounded like a lot of fun, especially if she could be in it with her best friend. Even though her best friend had been her best friend from the day she was born, sometimes her friend sort of forgot to act like a best friend. And Girl #1 couldn't help but think that this was one of those times.

So the night before the auditions, Girl #1 did the only thing that was left for her to do.

She went to the wish pond on her street. She found a perfect rock. She held it tightly in the palm of her hand and squeezed her eyes shut. Then she made a wish that she AND her friend would both get parts in the play at school.

She threw her rock in the water. As she walked home, she looked up at the night sky. When she found the brightest star, she repeated her wish again. Then she made her way home. One thing she was determined to do was get a good night's sleep before the big day.

She could only hope that her friend would be smart enough to do the same.

Girl #1 vs. Girl #2

Prepared   Not

AUDITIONS

Mom puts a plate of pancakes in front of me. "Saturday morning special," she says with a smile. "Today is a big day."

Mom is right. Tryouts for *Annie* are this morning.

I take a few bites of my pancakes and then push my plate back. "I'm too nervous to eat."

Mom wraps her arm around me. "You've spent so much time preparing. I know you'll do a wonderful job."

I think back to last night. I read the part Mr. Knight gave me for the audition and sang my song for Mom, Dad, and Max. Mom and Dad said I did a great job. Even Max, who said he'd practically gone deaf listening to me singing for the past week, said I sounded pretty good.

"I know I'm ready," I tell Mom. "But what I don't know is why I'm so nervous."

Mom kisses my forehead. "That's perfectly normal. In fact, it's good to be a little bit nervous. When you audition, all that extra energy will help you do an even better job than you did when you rehearsed at home."

"I hope you're right," I tell Mom. Then I look down at my plate.

"Mallory, is something else bothering you?" asks Mom.

I look up at the clock. I still have a few minutes before I need to go. "It's not me," I tell Mom. "It's Mary Ann." I explain to Mom how unenthusiastic Mary Ann has been about trying out for the play. "It's like she doesn't even care if she gets a part."

Mom opens her mouth like she is about to say something. Then she shuts it again and takes a deep breath. "Maybe Mary Ann has other things she is thinking about," says Mom.

I shrug my shoulders like that's not possible. "I don't know what else she would be thinking about. *Annie* is the only thing anyone at school is thinking about," I say in a dramatic voice.

Mom laughs. "Your voice was meant for the stage," she says. She stands up and gives me a hug like the conversation is over. "Good luck, Mallory. You'll do great."

I cross my toes and make a wish that Mom is right.

I walk out of my house and straight to the house next door to get Mary Ann, Winnie, and Joey. Mary Ann is trying out with me. Joey wants to sign up to be part of the crew, and Winnie wants to be in charge of makeup.

When I ring the doorbell, Joey and Winnie open the door. "Let's go," says Winnie. "I don't want to be late."

For once, I agree with Winnie completely. There's only one thing we're missing. "Where's Mary Ann?" I ask.

Winnie rolls her eyes. "She said something about watching *Fashion Fran*."

Winnie starts walking outside like she doesn't care if she leaves Mary Ann behind, but I do. I march into the den where Mary Ann is sitting on the couch. I pick up the remote and click off the TV. I like *Fashion Fran* as much as she does, but this is not the time to be watching her.

"C'mon. We'll be late for tryouts."

Mary Ann looks at me and shrugs. Then she gets up off the couch and walks toward the door without saying a word.

I know today is all about acting, but one thing Mary Ann is not doing is acting like Mary Ann. I wish she'd start acting more like her regular self who is always excited about everything. "Are you ready?" I ask her as we walk toward the auditorium.

"I don't know how she can be ready," says Winnie. "She barely rehearsed her lines. All she does lately is watch TV."

I ignore Winnie, and I hope Mary Ann does too. That's the last thing anyone who is about to audition for a show needs to hear.

I put my hand on Mary Ann's arm so she slows down. When Winnie and Joey are ahead of us, I give Mary Ann a little pep talk.

"I'm sure you're going to do great today."

"I guess so," says Mary Ann.

I put my arm around my friend. "You don't have to guess. I know you'll do great."

Mary Ann kind of half smiles, like half of her cares how she does at the auditions and the other half doesn't care at all.

"Don't forget that Mr. Knight said there will be parts for dancers too, and you are a really good dancer."

"Oh yeah," says Mary Ann like she had forgotten all about that.

I start to say more like, *"How could you forget you're a good dancer?"* But I don't get very far. "Hurry up!" says Joey. He holds the door open for us.

As we enter the auditorium, the director is already starting to talk. "Everyone come inside and find a seat," says a loud, clear voice from the stage. "If you're auditioning, please take a seat on the left. Those of you who want to be part of the crew, please find a seat on the right."

I look around as the left side of the auditorium fills up with kids from all grades.

"Over here!" Pamela motions to us to sit next to her. "I can't believe how many people are trying out," she says as we sit down.

"I think over half of the school is here," I say to Mary Ann and Pamela.

Mary Ann looks around the auditorium like she's taking it all in, but she doesn't say anything. I wish I had a crystal ball so I could see what's going on inside her head. I can't tell if she's nervous about the tryouts or if she doesn't care about the tryouts.

"Quiet, please!" The director smiles and waits while everyone settles down. "I'm Mrs. Denson, the drama teacher at Fern Falls Middle School. I'm going to be the director for this show, and I'm very excited as this is the first show we've done at the elementary school."

Lots of kids clap and cheer like they're just as excited as Mrs. Denson. And I'm one of them. Even though I haven't spent any time with Mrs. Denson, there's something about her big smile and friendly voice that makes me know I'm going to like her.

She asks everyone who is trying out to give her a few minutes while she talks to the kids who want to be part of the crew. When she's done signing everyone up for props, costumes, lighting, hair, and makeup, she excuses those kids and turns her attention to the other side of the room. Mrs. Denson claps her hands together. "Now, time for the actors," she says.

PROPS
everything onstage, except the scenery and the actors

"I have a list of all of you who signed up to audition. I will be calling on you in alphabetical order. When your name is called, please come up to the stage. I will ask you to recite the lines from the scene that you were given, and then you will have an opportunity to sing the song you have selected. Also, please let me know if you have any dance experience, and you are welcome to show me a few steps if you would like to."

SCENES
the "building blocks" of a play,
like chapters in a book

I take a deep breath as Mrs. Denson calls up a third grader, Samantha Adams.

"I'm glad our last names start with *M*. At least we don't have to go first," I whisper to Mary Ann.

Mary Ann gives a tiny nod. Usually she

would say something like, *"I'm so, so, so glad we don't have to go first."* But she doesn't say anything.

Maybe she's just nervous. I know I am. I feel like every bug, bird, and butterfly in Fern Falls is flying around in one place, and that one place is inside my stomach.

When Samantha finishes her song, Mrs. Denson calls on a boy from second grade. Pamela Brooks is next. I watch as kid after kid goes up on the stage to audition. Some are good, and some are not so good. I know it's not so nice to think this, but every time a *not-so-good* kid auditions, I feel like my chances of getting a part get a little better.

Mrs. Denson keeps going down the list. She calls up kids whose names start with *G*, *H*, *I*, *J*, and *K*. "We're almost to the *M*s," I whisper to Mary Ann.

We watch as Mrs. Denson calls up a boy from our class, Carlos Lopez, otherwise known as C-Lo and also Mary Ann's boyfriend.

As he walks up to the stage, I poke Mary Ann in the leg and wink at her. I know she'll be excited to watch him tryout. Mary Ann smiles a little, but it isn't her usual big, happy smile that she has when she sees C-Lo.

I start to say something to her like *"What is going on with you?"* or *"Did you forget to eat breakfast?"* or *"Are you really an alien who took over my best friend?"* But

I don't get to say anything because right when C-Lo finishes, Mrs. Denson calls out Mary Ann Martin.

I grab Mary Ann's arm. "Your turn. Good luck!" I whisper as she gets up.

I watch her walk up to the stage. Usually Mary Ann walks fast and she looks like she's dancing while she walks. But today, she looks like she's sleepwalking. I listen while she sings and recites her lines. She kind of seems like she's asleep while she does that too.

I think about all the kids who have tried out so far. Some were good, and some were not so good. Mary Ann didn't seem like she was either. She seemed like she wasn't even trying.

When Mrs. Denson asks Mary Ann if she has any dance experience, Mary Ann nods like she does but like it's no big deal. I want to stand up and say, *"Mary Ann is a great dancer! One time she performed hip-hop at the mall! Show her what you can do, Mary Ann!"*

But I don't say anything because as soon as Mary Ann is done, Mrs. Denson calls my name. As I run up to the stage, I try to push my thoughts about my best friend out of my brain.

When Mrs. Denson nods that she is ready for me to begin, I start reciting my monologue. At first, I feel nervous, but as I get into it, I feel better. By the time I get to my song, I feel good.

MONOLOGUE

a long speech by a single actor

When I'm done singing, Mrs. Denson smiles and nods like she approves.

"Great job!" lots of kids say as I walk back to my seat.

I take a deep breath as I sit down. I think about what Mom said about extra energy helping me do a good job. Maybe she was right. I felt good while I was auditioning, but it's hard to tell how I did. I remember the feeling of singing and reciting my lines, but I'm not sure what they sounded like coming out of my mouth.

"You sounded good," says Mary Ann like she can read my mind. For a minute, it's like she's the Mary Ann I know and love again.

I smile and mouth the words *thank you.* Even though I feel good about how I did, it's hard to feel completely happy because I don't feel good about how Mary Ann did. I look at her to see if she looks upset, but it's hard to tell how she's feeling.

It's also hard to sit and listen while the rest of the kids audition. All I want is to find out if I got a part and Mary Ann got a part. I cross my toes and hope that will happen.

"Good-bye, everyone," Mrs. Denson says when the last person is done. She waves a big, friendly wave. "Thanks to all of you for trying out. I will make casting decisions this week, and a cast list will be posted on the bulletin board in the cafeteria on Friday morning."

CAST
the actors chosen to perform in a play

As I walk home with Mary Ann, I start talking about the auditions.

"I can't believe how many kids tried out. There must have been over 100 kids. Or maybe over 200. Maybe even 1,000. I don't know. I don't think I could have counted all of those kids. I wonder how many will make it. I wonder who will get the big parts. I wonder how many kids will be in the chorus. Mrs. Denson seemed really nice. I think it would be tons of fun to be in the show. It is so cool that Fern Falls Elementary is putting on a show."

I go on and on about the auditions. When we get to Mary Ann's house, she touches my arm like we're at her stop. "See you later," she says.

I start walking to my house, but halfway there, I notice something. It's very quiet and not just because I stopped talking. Mary Ann didn't say a word the whole way home.

I walk back to the wish pond at the end of my street. I pick up a rock, close my eyes, and make a wish. Actually, I make two wishes.

I wish that I will get a part acting in the play.

I wish my best friend will start acting like herself.

PICKED!

When I wake up, I look at my calendar.

I'm glad I've already crossed off Monday,
Tuesday, Wednesday, and Thursday.
Those four days felt like four years.

It's finally Friday, and I don't know how
I've waited all week for it to get here.

I pop out of bed and put on the first
thing I pull out of my drawer. All I want
to do is get to school and see the cast list
that Mrs. Denson said she would post in the
cafeteria this morning.

I grab a doughnut and race next door. When I get to the Winstons', Joey and Winnie are already outside. "Hurry up!" says Winnie. "We were about to leave without you."

I feel like this is a repeat of audition day. "Where's Mary Ann?"

Joey points inside. I march into the house. I know she wouldn't be watching TV before school. I look in the kitchen first. I find Mary Ann staring into the toaster.

"C'mon," I say. "Don't you want to see if you got a part in the play?"

Mary Ann doesn't even look up at me. "I'm waiting for my bagel to toast."

When her bagel pops up, I grab it. "Let's go, you can eat it on the way."

"Don't you think it would be fun if we both got parts in the play?" I ask as we walk to school.

Mary Ann nods, but I don't think it's a *yes-it-would-be-fun* nod. It's more of an *I-can't-talk-because-my-mouth-is-full-of-bagel* nod.

I don't say anything else to Mary Ann. I don't know why she's acting so weird lately. And right now, I don't have time to figure it out. "C'mon!" I say as we walk through the school gates. I grab her bagel-free hand and run to the cafeteria. All I want to do is see the cast list.

I guess I'm not the only one who wants to see if they got a part in *Annie*. The cafeteria is jam-packed with kids from every grade.

Everyone is crowded around the bulletin board.

I squeeze Mary Ann's hand, and we make our way toward the front of the crowd so we can see what other people are already looking at.

I hear lots of *oooh*s and *aah*s and *I can't believe I made it*s!

I cross my toes that I'll be saying the same sort of thing.

"Have you seen the list yet?" Arielle asks as I push past her.

I shake my head that I haven't. She gives me a look, but I can't tell if it's a *you-want-to-see-the-list* look or a *you-don't-want-to-see-the-list* look. I try to swallow, but I feel like one of the cafeteria trays is stuck in my throat.

When I finally get to the front of the room, I start reading the list. Joey is the stage manager. I skim through the rest of the crew. What I really want to see is who will be in the cast of *Annie.*

But as soon as I see the cast list, I stop and rub my eyes. I can't believe what I'm seeing. The first name on the list is mine. I'm playing the part of Annie!

I've never even been in a play before, and Mrs. Denson picked me to play the lead!

THE LEAD
actor or actress who has the main part

"Mallory, I'm one of the orphans!" screams my friend April, who is standing next to me.

"We're orphans too!" scream two third-grade girls.

"So am I!" says Danielle. "And so is Arielle. We're the head orphans."

"I'm Miss Hannigan, the lady in charge of the orphanage," screams Pamela.

We all start jumping up and down. Before I know it lots of people who got picked are jumping up and down with us.

But there's someone who isn't jumping.

I stop and start looking at the list again. "Let's find your name," I say to Mary Ann.

I start at the top and read down. I get to the bottom of the list, but I don't see Mary Ann's name. All that jumping must have done something to my reading skills. I start again at the top of the list and go slowly this time. I still don't see Mary Ann's name anywhere.

I try to swallow, but now I feel like I have two cafeteria trays and a vending machine stuck in my throat. Mary Ann's name isn't anywhere.

Even though Mary Ann didn't seem very enthusiastic when she auditioned, I thought she would at least get a part. I look at the names listed under *Chorus*

again. There are a lot of names, and hers has to be there somewhere.

"I didn't make it," Mary Ann says.

Even though I feel so happy about being the lead, I feel so unhappy that Mary Ann won't be in the play with me. It would have been so much fun to practice our lines together and go to all the rehearsals.

Mary Ann shrugs like she doesn't care that she didn't make it. "It's no big deal. It's just a play." She picks up her backpack and starts to leave the cafeteria.

"Yeah," I say like she's right. But the thing is, I can't tell if she thinks it's a big deal or not. Lately, I can't tell much of anything when it comes to Mary Ann.

ACTING WEIRD

If you ask me, I'm not the only one on Wish Pond Road who's been spending a lot of time acting lately. Even though Mary Ann is not in the play and doesn't have any lines to learn or any rehearsals to attend, she's spending more time acting than I am.

And the way she has been acting is weird.

Even though I never talk to Max about anything serious, last night while Max was brushing his teeth, I tried talking to him about it.

I told him that Mary Ann has been acting weird lately, and he said she always acts weird. But I told him that wasn't what I was talking about.

I gave him five examples of exactly what I was talking about.

WEIRD EXAMPLE #1: AT A SLEEPOVER

Last weekend, after we found out who got parts in the play and who didn't, Mary Ann and I had a sleepover, and she did something very weird: she slept!

One thing Mary Ann and I never do at a sleepover is sleep. We usually stay up all night talking and laughing. We usually get in lots of trouble because Mom has to come in my room about ten times before we finally turn the lights and our mouths off.

But that's not what happened at our last sleepover. At our last sleepover, Mary Ann and I barely talked at all. At first, all Mary Ann wanted to do was watch TV. Then she said she wanted to read.

That's right. Mary Ann brought a book, and she said she wanted to read it. So she sat and read on one side of my bed, and I sat and pretended to read on the other. When she said she was done reading, she said she wanted to go to sleep. Weird, huh?

WEIRD EXAMPLE #2: ONE DAY AFTER REHEARSALS

On Tuesday after rehearsals, I stopped by Mary Ann's house. (You're probably wondering how a girl who is the star in a play has time to stop by someone's house when she is busy with rehearsals. Well, that's a good question and here's the answer: I made time.)

That's right. Even though my life is totally busy with rehearsals every day after school, I stopped by Mary Ann's house to say hi and to see if she wanted to watch *Fashion Fran* together. I even got Mom to help me bake cookies, and I took them over there. I thought I was being very nice to do this. Mary Ann has been my best friend since the day I was born, and I didn't want her to think that I  thought I was better than her just because I'm the star of a play and she's not.

But guess what? When I went to her house, Mary Ann said she didn't want to watch *Fashion Fran* because she had to do her homework AND she said she didn't

want any cookies because she is trying not
to eat sweets.

   I asked Max if he thought that seemed
weird. But Max said that didn't seem
weird to him. He said everyone has to do

What's wrong with my friend?

Time to study. | None for me.

SICK? | It's a mystery.

homework sometimes and that Mary Ann probably didn't want the cookies because she was afraid to eat anything I baked.

But I said it was weird because (a) Mary Ann never does homework and (b) she will eat anything that anyone bakes (even me).

WEIRD EXAMPLE #3: IN THE LUNCHROOM

On Thursday at lunch, I sat down at the table where I always sit with my friends. I always bring my lunch, so I get to the table before Mary Ann gets there because she always buys her lunch. I always save her a seat next to me, and she always sits in it.

BUT NOT ON THURSDAY.

On Thursday she bought her lunch and then she sat at another table with her boyfriend, C-Lo. I wanted to remind her that even though C-Lo is her boyfriend, he is NOT who she eats lunch with. I AM!

But since she was already halfway through her lunch before I thought about saying it, I decided instead to tell Pamela how weird it was, and she agreed that it was unbelievably, totally weird.

WEIRD EXAMPLE #4: ON THE WAY TO SCHOOL

One of the weirdest things that Mary Ann has ever done happened on Friday. Mary Ann walked to school without me. Mary Ann never walks to school without me! EVER!

Every single day, she waits for me and we walk to school together. But on Friday, she didn't do that.

She went to school, and I saw her when I got there. And get this . . . she didn't even say anything to me like, "Sorry I didn't wait for you."

In fact, she barely said anything to me the whole day. If you ask me, that's kind of like ignoring me, so I did the only thing that was left for me to do. Tonight after dinner, I sent her an email asking her what's going on and why she's been acting so weird lately, and that's when she did the weirdest thing of all.

WEIRD EXAMPLE #5: AN EMAIL I SENT TO MARY ANN

Subject: Why are you acting so weird?
From: malgal
To: chatterbox

Dear Mary Ann,

I'm writing you an email because lately it seems like you have been acting weird.

I don't mean weird in a bad way. I mean weird in a not yourself way. Do you know what I mean? Anyway, maybe it is something you ate in the cafeteria, like vegetables. I have heard of that happening. It's why I like to stick to peanut butter and marshmallow sandwiches. Maybe from now on, you can bring your lunch to school instead of buying it and you will go back to acting like yourself. Don't you think that is a good idea?

OK. See you tomorrow (when hopefully you will be acting like yourself again).

Mallory

When I finished writing the email, I sent it to Mary Ann. Then I waited for her to write back, but she didn't.

Mary Ann never wrote.

How totally weird is that? Mary Ann always writes back.

Now you know why I did something weird myself. (I'm talking about talking to Max.)

When I finished giving Max all the examples of Mary Ann's weird behavior, all he said was that if it was anyone else, he would think it was weird. But since it is Mary Ann, he thinks it is totally normal.

Well, I did NOT agree and I told Max that I have a theory about why Mary Ann is acting so weird.

Max snorted (not a pretty sound) and said he couldn't wait to hear my theory.

So I told him that I think the reason Mary Ann is acting so weird is because she is jealous of my theatrical success.

When I said that, Max stopped snorting and started laughing. Really hard. He said that was one of the most ridiculous things he had ever heard and that now he knows why Mary Ann and I are friends. He said we are both weird.

But I'm not so sure about that.

The more I think about it, what I am sure about is that my *My-Best-Friend-Acting-Weird-Because-She-Is-Jealous* theory

might not be so far from wrong.

FRIENDS & FAMILY

"Places, everyone. Today's rehearsal is all about knowing your lines," says Mrs. Denson.

She wants everyone *off book*. She says that is the technical term for not relying on the script. The show is in two weeks, and even though everyone is doing a good job learning the lines and songs, we still have a lot of rehearsing to do.

Especially me. Having the lead role in a show sounds like a lot of fun, and it has been, but it's been a lot of work too.

"Mallory, are you ready?" Joey has a copy of the script in one hand. As stage manager, he's in charge of making sure everyone has what they need onstage. He has his dog Murphy's leash in the other hand. In the play, Annie has a dog named Sandy and Murphy is playing Sandy.

I pat Murphy on the head. "I hope I can remember all of my lines."

Joey smiles at me. "If you forget something, just call for a line."

I nod, but I hope I don't have to. *Calling for a line* is the term Mrs. Denson taught us for when you're onstage and forget what you're supposed to say. Just hearing Joey say it makes me feel like a real actress.

"Orphans over here," shouts Mrs. Denson.

All the orphans, led by Arielle and Danielle, take their places at the center of the stage. Mrs. Denson wants them to rehearse their dances first.

I sit next to Joey and Murphy on the side of the stage and watch while the orphans dance.

I can't help thinking about Mary Ann and how much fun it would have been if she had been in the show. She is a really good dancer. I wish she had tried harder at auditions. She could have been one of the orphans too.

When the orphans finish their dances, Mrs. Denson tells everyone to take their places backstage. "We're going to start at the beginning and go all the way through the show today," she says.

BACKSTAGE
any part of the stage not in the acting area

When she signals for us to start, I watch as one of the orphans says the opening lines. Then it is my turn. I walk out on the stage. I'm always a little bit scared to begin with, but once I do, it's amazing how quickly I start to feel more like Annie than like Mallory.

As we go through the show, Mrs. Denson gives lots of directions.

Mallory, over here. Orphans, over there. Everyone, speak up, speak slowly. Use your stage voices.

Joey works from the side of the stage feeding lines to whoever forgets them. The good news is that I'm not one of those people. Even though I have everything memorized, it's still hard to remember it all when you go through the whole show. Now I know why actors rehearse a lot before a show.

"Everyone, take a break," Mrs. Denson yells from the front of the auditorium. "We're halfway through the show. You have five minutes. When I call you, please be prepared to finish rehearsing."

Arielle and Danielle follow me as I walk backstage. "Mallory, you're doing a great job as Annie," says Arielle.

Danielle smiles and nods. "Really great!"

"Thanks!" I tell them. They almost never have anything nice to say. It makes me feel good when they do, especially this. "I'm trying hard."

Arielle nods. "It's totally obvious." Then she gets a funny look on her face like there's something else that isn't so obvious. "I haven't seen you and Mary Ann together much lately."

I shrug like I don't know what to say, and the truth is, I don't. Mary Ann and I haven't been together much lately, but I'm not sure I want to talk to Arielle and Danielle about it.

"Yeah," says Danielle. "You guys are like best friends, and best friends always hang together." Danielle slips her arm through Arielle's. "We're best friends, and we're always together."

Danielle is right. Best friends are supposed to hang together.

"I've noticed that she doesn't even sit with you at lunch," says Arielle.

I pick a fuzz ball off my sweater.

Maybe I can talk to Arielle and Danielle about it . . . just a little bit.

"Ever since we started play practice, she hasn't been sitting with me at lunch or walking with me to school or even talking to me very much," I say.

Danielle slips her free arm through mine like now Arielle, Danielle, and I are a threesome. "Why do you think Mary Ann is acting so weird?" She makes a face like she's just as upset about the way Mary Ann is acting as I must be.

I shrug again and scratch my neck.

Joey looks at me from the other side of the stage. He gives me a *why-in-the-world-are-you-arm-and-arm-with-Arielle-and-Danielle* look.

It seems like Arielle and Danielle are trying to be nice, but I'm not sure I should say anything else about Mary Ann.

I look at Mrs. Denson to see if she is ready to call the actors back onstage yet, but she is busy talking to the kids who are in the lighting box.

"So?" says Arielle like she's waiting for my answer.

"You must have some idea." Danielle smiles at me. "Now that we're in the same cast, we're practically like family. You can tell us anything."

I never thought of a cast being like a family, but in a way, it is.

I look across the stage at Joey, but he is busy talking to the kids who are doing lighting. Maybe it will be good to talk to Arielle and Danielle about what's been happening and why Mary Ann has been acting so weird lately.

I take a deep breath. "It just seems like things with Mary Ann have been different ever since this whole play thing started."

I pause.

Arielle looks at me like I should go on, so I do.

"When I got the lead and she didn't get a part, it seems like she kind of quit talking to me. You know, like maybe she got jealous or something."

Arielle and Danielle look at each other. Then they look at me like they understand exactly what I'm talking about.

"Time to start," calls out Mrs. Denson.

Joey motions for cast members to find their places onstage.

When Arielle and Danielle are with the other orphans on center stage, he walks over to where I'm standing. "It looks like you were having a deep conversation with Arielle and Danielle." His voice is a little sharper than usual like he doesn't approve.

"It was no big deal," I say. "We were just talking."

"I don't trust them," says Joey. "And I don't think you should either." He gives me a serious look. "Even though you're in the same show, it doesn't mean they're your friends."

I think about what Danielle said about a cast being like a family. Ever since we started play rehearsals, Arielle and Danielle have been nice. It seems like they want to be my friends.

"Places," says Mrs. Denson.

Joey gives me a *the-conversation-is-over-but-I-hope-you'll-think-about-what-I-said* look.

I watch as he gives the orphans the cue to start their next song.

CUE

a signal that starts a change of any kind during a performance

I'd like to give Joey a cue to stick to his job as stage manager, not friend manager.

A LETTER

From: Mrs. Denson, Director
To: Cast Members and Crew of *Annie*
Subject: Final Week

Dear Cast and Crew,

Congratulations on making it to the final week before the big performance. As Friday night is showtime, we have a lot to do this week to be ready. The following are a few last-minute instructions for all of you to follow:

REHEARSALS: We will be rehearsing Monday, Tuesday, and Wednesday at our regular time after school. As these are our final rehearsals, it is important that everyone comes ready to work.

COSTUMES: All the costumes are ready (and look fantastic)! They will be backstage and ready for you when you arrive for dress rehearsal.

DRESS REHEARSAL: Dress rehearsal begins promptly on Thursday at 5:30 p.m. in the auditorium. Please have a snack beforehand. (Actors do better with food in their stomachs!) We will do a straight run-through of the whole show.

PERFORMANCE NIGHT: Everyone needs to be backstage for costumes and makeup at 5:30 sharp! The show starts at 7:00, but we will need plenty of time for last-minute adjustments.

NERVES: You have all worked so hard. It's normal to be nervous right before a performance. Just remember: if you forget a line or aren't sure where your place is on the stage, our crew members will be there on the sides of the stage to help you. And here's a tip: don't forget to breathe! Repeat after me: breathe deep! I promise, it helps.

I know you will all do a great job. It has been a pleasure working with each and every one of you, and I can't wait until the big night!

Mrs. Denson

D IS FOR "DRAMA"

D is also for "dress rehearsal," which happens to be starting in a few minutes. I watch Joey hand out costumes.

As I button my dress, I think about the last few weeks of rehearsals. I can't believe the show is tomorrow night.

Max says he can't wait for it to get here. He says he is tired of listening to me sing in the shower every morning.

For once, I agree with Max. I can't wait for the show to get here either. Everyone in the cast has been working so hard. We all know our songs and dances and lines. The only thing left to do is have a good dress rehearsal, and then we will be ready to go.

DRESS REHEARSAL
rehearsal in costumes prior
to the real thing

I tie my apron around my waist. Then I close my eyes and make a wish. *I wish everything will go smoothly from now until the show is over.*

I've heard of weird things happening to actresses right before they get ready to perform. I heard about one who mysteriously lost her voice and another who found a rare white frog in her toilet and missed her performance because she wanted to take the frog to the zoo.

I don't want to lose my voice, find any animals, or have anything out of the ordinary happen to me before the show.

Mrs. Denson claps her hands together like she wants our attention. "Everyone, please check your costumes to make sure you have on everything you're supposed to be wearing. Joey is going to come around with the prop list and make sure you all have your props."

Mrs. Denson clears her throat like what she is about to say is important. "Once we get started, we are going to go through the whole show. If you forget a line,

Joey will feed it to you. If you get stuck, improvise. I want you to pretend that this is the real thing."

When everyone is dressed and ready, Mrs. Denson smiles at us and bows. "Places everyone. The Fern Falls Elementary production of *Annie* is about to begin."

I wait for my cue to go on after the orphans begin. I walk to the spot marked with an *X* in the middle of the stage. When I get there, I look out at where the audience will be seated like I'm sad. That's what the script says I am supposed to do. Then I begin my first song.

Mrs. Denson nods like she approves.

When I'm done singing, Pamela takes her place and sings her song. She is really funny. She was a good choice to play Miss Hannigan.

One by one, we go through all the scenes and songs and dances in the play. Partway through the show, I do a costume change from my orphan dress to what Ms. Denson calls my "Annie" dress.

Everyone does a really good job with the lines and songs and dances. Even Murphy sits and stays and follows me when he is supposed to.

When the whole cast is done with the last song, we all take a bow the way Mrs. Denson taught us to do when the show is over. Before we have a chance to run offstage and come back on for final bows, Mrs. Denson starts clapping.

"Bravo!" she says in her loud, clear voice. "That was a terrific performance. I think the show will go very well tomorrow night. You can all give your props and costumes back to Joey. He is going to have everything organized and ready to go tomorrow night." Mrs. Denson is all smiles as she gives us final instructions for tomorrow night's performance.

I can tell she is pleased, and so am I.

"Mallory, you were great," says April.

Pamela nods like she agrees.

"Fantastic!" says Arielle.

Danielle gives me a big hug like she thinks so too.

"Thanks!" I squeeze Murphy. "You did a good job too," I tell him.

Arielle laughs like the idea of telling a dog he did a good job is funny in a good way. Danielle pats Murphy on the back.

Mrs. Denson tells us all to go home and have a nice, relaxing night, which is what I am planning to do.

"Bye!" Arielle waves to me as I leave the auditorium with Joey.

Danielle crosses her fingers in a good luck sign. "I know you'll do great tomorrow."

"It seems like Arielle and Danielle are your new best friends," Joey says as we walk home.

"They've been nice lately," I say to Joey. "It's been fun being in the play with them."

Joey frowns like even though they have been nicer than usual, he doesn't really trust their niceness. "Speaking of friends, I haven't seen much of you and Mary Ann together lately."

Now it's my turn to frown. With dress rehearsal today, I haven't had much time to think about things with Mary Ann. "I've just been busy," I tell Joey.

What I don't tell him is that I'm pretty sure it's more than that. I think about the conversation I had last week at rehearsals with Arielle and Danielle. I don't want to tell Joey I think Mary Ann is jealous of me.

As we cross by the wish pond on our street, I make a wish. Even though I've already made this wish, I can't help wishing for it again. *I wish when the play is over that things will go back to normal with Mary Ann.*

When we pass in front of the Winstons', Joey waves bye and I walk to my house.

When I get inside, I take a deep breath. "Something smells terrific," I say.

Mom smiles. "Dinner will be ready soon. In honor of our actress, we're having spaghetti and meatballs."

"Mmmm!" My favorite. I can't wait to eat. While Mom is chopping the salad, I turn on the computer in the kitchen. When I do, I see that I have an email. The only thing better than my favorite dinner is getting mail. I click on it.

Subject: Someone Not in the Play
From: dancergirl1, dancergirl2
To: malgal

Hi Mallory. (Or should we say Annie?!?) We just wanted to write and make sure our star is OK. We wanted to talk to you today to see if things are better with a certain someone not in the play. (In case your brain is too filled up with lines and lyrics, we are talking about Mary Ann.) We hope she will do what a good best friend should do, which is call you tonight (or better yet, bring you flowers and candy) to wish you good luck in tomorrow night's performance. If she doesn't, you can tell us and we will bring you flowers ourselves.

Love and kisses (and flowers),
Arielle and Danielle

"Time for dinner," Mom says when I'm done reading.

As I click off the email, I can't help thinking about what Arielle and Danielle wrote. They are right. Mary Ann is my best friend, and tomorrow is a big day for me. Flowers and candy would be great, but she should at least call me or come over. She has barely said a word to me all week.

I look at the clock on the computer. Maybe Mary Ann is waiting until after dinner to wish me luck.

At dinner, everyone in my family wants to talk about the play. I hope they're not the only ones on Wish Pond Road that want to talk about it. When I'm done with my spaghetti and meatballs, I look at the clock.

Still no Mary Ann.

I do my homework.

No Mary Ann.

I eat dessert. I take a bath. I brush my teeth, and I even floss them.

Still no Mary Ann.

I take a deep breath, which smells like toothpaste. Usually a fresh mouth makes me feel happy, but right now, what I feel is mad. I hate to think the thoughts that are going through my head, but I can't help it.

Even though part of me understands why Mary Ann would be jealous, the other part of me feels like she didn't even try to get a part. She should at least be happy for me that I did.

"Can I have five minutes?" I ask when Mom says it is time for bed.

When she says yes, I run to the kitchen. I click on the email I got from Arielle and Danielle. They are acting like better friends than Mary Ann.

I hit *reply.*

Subject: Flowers and Candy
From: malgal
To: dancergirl1, dancergirl2

Arielle and Danielle,

Guess what . . . no flowers or candy or phone calls or visits. You heard right. Mary Ann didn't even send me an email to say good luck. She didn't send anything. Even though she has been my best friend since the day I was born, she isn't acting like one. The only thing she is acting like is a BAD friend, and I know it is because she is jealous. J-E-A-L-O-U-S. I am sure Mary Ann is jealous of me because I am the star in the show and she is nothing. N-O-T-H-I-N-G. Oh well. I guess there's N-O-T-H-I-N-G I can do about it. Thanks for being such good friends.

Mallory

P.S. I.C.W.U.S.! (Short for *I can't wait until showtime!*)

P.P.S. You don't have to bring me flowers and candy. (OK. Maybe a little candy would be nice.)

When I'm done writing, I push the *send* button, and I feel better when I do. Then I push all thoughts of my best friend who isn't acting like one out of my brain.

I close my eyes when Mom kisses me good night. I want to get a good night's sleep. Tomorrow is one of the biggest days of my life, and I don't want anything to ruin it.

A TALE OF TWO FRIENDS: PART 2

So the tale of the two friends continues as Girl #1 stands backstage, ready to go on the night of the biggest performance of her life. But something was troubling her. Her best friend (remember Girl #2, the one who had been acting weird lately) still hadn't wished her good luck before the show. In fact, she hadn't said one word to her all day.

Girl #1 peered out into the theater. She saw Girl #2. She waved to her, but Girl #2 didn't wave back. Even though Girl #1 didn't think she should be the one to do this, she went to say a quick hello to her friend. But when Girl #1 got to where Girl #2 was sitting, some very strange things happened.

Girl #2 didn't look like she was happy to see Girl #1. Not only did she not wish her luck in the show, she actually said that the only reason she even came was because her mother made her come.

Girl #1 was confused. She told Girl #2 that she didn't understand why she was acting this way.

So Girl #2 shoved something into Girl #1's hand. It was a piece of paper.

Unsure what was on the piece of paper, Girl #1 did what anyone would do

who wanted
to know what
was on a piece
of paper. She
looked at it.
But when she
did, she didn't
like what she
saw. On the
piece of paper
was an email.

It took a minute for Girl #1's brain to
fully understand why Girl #2 had a copy
of this email. It was an email that Girl #1
had written about Girl #2. She knew she
hadn't sent it to Girl #2, but then, without
having to think for another second, she
knew exactly who had.

Her friends (if you can call them
that) whose names start with an A

and a D must have sent her email to Girl #2.

That's right. They sent something that was sent to them to someone who wasn't supposed to see it.

When Girl #1 realized what had happened, at first she got angry and her mind filled with questions.

How could those girls have done something like that? Was it illegal to do something like that? Could they go to jail (and if they did, who would play their parts in the show)? Why would they have done something like that if they were her friends?

As all of these questions ran through Girl #1's brain, she realized she felt sick (not feverish sick or like she needed to blow her nose sick but sick in every part of her body). Sick from the top of her head to the tip of her toes but especially sick in her stomach.

She was mad at the girls who sent the email, but she knew that wasn't going to help anything with her best friend.

What she had written didn't sound very nice. She knew it must have been why her best friend was so upset. She started to say something, but before the words could come out of her mouth, Girl #2 stood up and ran out of the theater.

Girl #1 knew she had to find her best friend and talk to her. She could feel the tears starting to spill down her cheeks. She looked down at the piece of paper in her hand and wished she could take it all back or, at the very least, magically turn it into a tissue.

Would her best friend still want to be her best friend?

She closed her eyes and made a wish that the answer to that last question would be yes. All she wanted to do was run out of the theater and find her friend and talk to her, but she knew she couldn't do that. The show was about to begin.

THE SHOW MUST GO ON

"Places, everyone!" Joey looks serious as he points at the orphans to move to the back of the stage, behind the curtain.

Winnie runs around with a powder puff, putting the finishing touches of makeup on all the actors. Some of the crew members do a final sound check.

"Mallory, are you ready?" Joey asks. "As soon as Mrs. Denson finishes her welcoming speech, the curtain is going up. The orphans will do their opening scene, and then it's your turn."

I wipe my eyes and nod like I'm ready to play Annie. But I don't feel like Annie at all. Annie in the show is nice and bighearted. Annie always tries to help her friends. I feel like Mallory. Sick, sad, bad Mallory who writes mean emails about her friend.

I listen from backstage as Mrs. Denson tells the audience how excited she is to present the first-ever school play at Fern Falls

Portrait of a terrible friend

Elementary. She says that each and every member of the cast and crew has worked hard.

I look at Arielle and Danielle, who are at the front of the group of orphans. I can't even believe they sent Mary Ann a copy of the email I wrote. I know I shouldn't have written it, but I don't know why they sent it to her. They are both smiling like nothing is wrong, and they can't wait to perform. I can't believe I thought they were my friends.

Joey taps me on the shoulder as Mrs. Denson tells the audience how much she has enjoyed working with all of us and how proud she is to present *Annie*.

When the curtain rises, the orphans start the show with the opening scene.

"Your turn!" Joey whispers to me when they are done. He points me toward the stage.

I don't know how I'm going to think like Annie when all I can think about is finding Mary Ann and telling her how sorry I am I wrote that email.

I walk to the *X* on the center of the stage floor. When I get there, I look sad. Not because it's what it says I'm supposed to do in the script. I look sad because I am sad.

The audience claps. I guess they think I am a very good actress to be able to make myself look so sad, but it isn't hard.

I stand there looking sad for a long time.

I hear the music begin. That is my cue to start singing. I open my mouth, but my song does not come out.

I can hear Joey singing the words from the side of the stage. I know he wants me to start singing with him, but all of a sudden, I feel like that actress I read about.

I can't find my voice. This is not supposed to be happening. All I can think about is Mary Ann never talking to me again. I can't imagine my life without her as my best friend. I feel hot tears starting to make little puddles in the corners of my eyes.

Joey stops the music. He motions to me that we are going to start again. "Sing with me," he mouths.

The audience is quiet, like they know this is not how the play goes. I look at the audience to see if Mary Ann came back, but the lights are so bright, I can't tell who anyone is. If I could find her and talk to her, I think I could start singing.

I can hear the music starting again.

All of my life, Mary Ann has always been there when I need to talk to her, and now—when I really need to—she's not, and it's my fault that she isn't.

Joey is waving to me and mouthing the words from the side of the stage. But I don't sing along with him. I can't. It's like I forgot every single line I'm supposed to sing.

The music stops again. As loud as the applause was a few minutes ago is how quiet the auditorium is now. I know the audience knows something is wrong, and I know they know something is wrong with me.

Mrs. Denson looks at me like she can't imagine why I'm not singing. She motions for me to start.

I see her talking to Joey, and he shrugs his shoulders like he does not know what to do.

But I do. I know what I have to do.

I can hear everyone in the audience whispering as I walk offstage. I wish this wasn't happening, but there's no way I can be Annie when all I can think about is being Mallory.

Mrs. Denson is at my side as soon as I walk backstage. "Mallory, are you OK?" She looks concerned.

"What's going on?" asks Joey.

I shake my head like I don't want to talk

Portrait of a stage manager with no clue what to do

about it. "There's no time to explain," I say to Joey. "But I can't go back onstage until you find Mary Ann and bring her backstage."

Everyone in the cast is starting to crowd around me.

"Mallory, are you sick?" asks April.

Pamela looks confused.

Winnie gives me an impatient look. "Get back out there. Your makeup is fine."

"What's going on?" asks Arielle as if she doesn't like it that something is stopping her from dancing onstage.

"We demand to know what's going on!" says Danielle.

I really don't want to tell anyone what happened. I give Joey an *I-wouldn't-have-asked-you-to-find-Mary Ann-if-I-didn't-need-her* look.

Joey nods like he gets it and hands me Murphy's leash. "I'll be right back," he says.

Joey is gone before anyone has a chance to ask what's going on.

I take a deep breath. I know this isn't how tonight was supposed to happen. Everything was supposed to go smoothly, just like it did at dress rehearsal.

Mrs. Denson gives me a very serious look. "Mallory, you may have a few minutes, but the show must go on."

I look at the clock on the wall and pretend like it's the wish pond. I close my eyes and make a wish, actually two.

I wish Joey will find Mary Ann and bring her here, and I wish he will do it quickly.

LIGHTS, CAMERA, ACTION

"Mary Ann!"

I scream her name and run to hug her as soon as Joey walks backstage with her. I've never been so happy to see my best friend. The only problem is that she doesn't look as happy to see me. In fact, I think if Joey weren't holding her arm so tightly, she'd probably turn around and leave.

Mrs. Denson gives me an *if-this-is-what-you-need-to-start-acting-like-Annie* look, hurry up! I don't mind conflict on stage, but I don't like it in real life. I take a deep breath and start talking.

CONFLICT

the struggle between two or more actors that leads to a climax

"Mary Ann, I'm so sorry about the email," I whisper as I pull my friend over to a corner. I don't want anyone else to hear what I have to say.

Mary Ann starts to talk, but I stop her before she starts. "Wait, there are some things I have to say to you."

I tell Mary Ann that I never meant to write an email about her, especially to Arielle and Danielle, and that I shouldn't

have written it, and there is no excuse for
writing it, and I'm totally sorry I wrote it,
but I did because lately she hasn't been
acting like my best friend, and Arielle and
Danielle have been nice since we start
rehearsing together, and I should have
known that even when they're acting nice,
they're not really nice, and I feel terrible
that I trusted them and wrote something
bad about her that probably isn't even
true, and I hope she can forgive me

because I would be so, so, so upset if she wasn't my best friend.

When I finish, I take a deep breath and look at Mary Ann. I hope she will say something like, *"Mallory, I totally forgive you. You are my best, best, best friend and always will be."*

But that's not what she says. "Mallory, I can't believe you wrote an email about me to Arielle and Danielle. I know we always say things three times, but when I saw your email, I had to read it three times. I couldn't believe you wrote it. I'm your best friend. We've been best friends since we were born. I can't believe you thought I was jealous of you."

I look down at my shoes and tights. Listening to Mary Ann, I don't know how I ever thought she was jealous. My costume is starting to feel hot and itchy. I look up at Mary Ann. "I'm really sorry about what I wrote, and I'm even sorrier that I thought you were jealous. It's just that you weren't acting like yourself at all and that was the only thing that seemed different."

Mary Ann is quiet for a minute like she's thinking.

"Mallory, I have something to tell you." Even though we are alone in the corner, she looks around like she wants to make absolutely sure no one can hear her. Then she leans over and whispers in my ear.

As she whispers, I nod, like I am listening to every word that she is saying, and I am. When she is done talking, I look at her. I can't believe what I just heard. It explains a lot about why she hasn't been acting like herself lately.

"Are you sure?" I ask Mary Ann.

She nods her head that she is.

Wow! I start to say something to her, but Mrs. Denson interrupts me. "Ladies, are we done here?"

Mary Ann smiles at me. Then she gives me a big hug.

Even though she hasn't said that she forgives me, I know she has.

"We can talk about it more later," says Mary Ann. "You have a show to put on."

Now it is my turn to smile. "I think I'm ready to be Annie," I tell Mrs. Denson.

She nods that she's glad to hear this. "Places, everyone!" says Mrs. Denson. She signals to Joey that it is curtain time.

"Break a leg!" Mary Ann mouths to me.

When I walk back out onto the stage, the audience claps. I try to look sad, but this time it isn't so easy.

I'm glad when the music starts. After just a few lines of my song, I feel like Annie.

When I'm done singing, Pamela comes onstage and sings her song as Miss Hannigan.

We go through the rest of the show just like we did at dress rehearsal, only this time, it's even better. Everyone is loud and clear. We use our stage voices just like Mrs. Denson taught us to do. No one misses any words of their songs or any steps in their dances. Even Murphy barks when he is supposed to.

Mrs. Denson told us there is something magical about being in front of an audience, and now, I think I know what she means. It was so much work rehearsing the show, and now, it all feels worth it. It's exciting to be onstage, and I can tell

everyone in the cast feels it too.

When the whole cast finishes the final song, we all take a bow. The audience stands up and claps. Lots of people whistle and shout. I've never heard so much noise in the auditorium.

It was so much fun acting in the play, but it's even more fun being done acting in a play. I'm so happy that it went well.

Joey motions for the cast to run off the stage.

We do, and then we start going up in groups for our final bows, or *curtain call*, which Mrs. Denson said is the official term.

First, the chorus goes up, then the orphans, and then all the individual actors. Then everyone in the crew joins them onstage. Since I'm the star, I go last with Murphy. When I get to the middle of the stage, I take a deep bow, I hug Murphy, and he wags his tail like he's happy too. The audience claps even louder.

EXIT
when everyone leaves the stage

We all take one final bow before we exit. The first-ever play at Fern Falls Elementary is officially over, and if you ask me, it was a big hit.

A TALE OF TWO FRIENDS: PART 3

The tale of the two friends continues...

The minute that the play was over, Girl #1 ran out from behind the curtain. Though she enjoyed her time onstage playing someone else, all she wanted to do was to be herself again. She couldn't get it out of her mind what Girl #2 had told her right before the show, and she couldn't wait to find her and talk to her.

She searched desperately through the crowd until she found her friend. She was with her mother. Even though they were in an auditorium filled with people, it looked like Girl #2 and her mother were both crying.

Girl #1 ran to Girl #2 and threw her arms around her neck.

"Are you OK? Is it really true?" Girl #1 asked Girl #2.

But before Girl #2 had a chance to answer, Girl #2's mother answered for her.

"Yes, Mallory. (That is what Girl #1.)

Girl #1 hugging Girl #2

Frank and I are having a baby. Mary Ann is going to be a big sister."

Before Girl #1 could say anything else like "WOW! MARY ANN (that is what Girl #1 sometimes called Girl #2) IS GOING TO BE A BIG SISTER!" or "Why was it such a big secret?" or "How come Mary Ann didn't want to tell me?" Girl #2's mother kept talking.

Blah
Blah
Blah
Blah
Blah

Portrait of a pregnant lady who really likes to talk.

"Mary Ann said she told you about the baby. I didn't know she knew. She overheard Frank and me talking. But we wanted to talk to Mary Ann, Joey, and Winnie at the same time."

Girl #1 tried to listen while Girl #2's mother was explaining things, but she was having a hard time listening because she was busy watching a tear (actually lots of them) roll down Girl #2's cheeks. She realized that the reason Girl #2 hadn't been interested in the play was because she had other, bigger things to think about, like becoming a big sister.

"Are you sad about the baby?" Girl #1 asked her friend.

"Not sad," said Girl #2 in a little voice. "But maybe a little bit scared."

Girl #1 noticed that when Girl #2 said what she did about being scared, she kind of looked like a baby herself.

"Mary Ann told me she is scared about what this will mean for her," said Girl #2's mother. Then she put her arm around her daughter and planted a big kiss right on her forehead (even though she was still in the auditorium filled with tons of people). "But I told Mary Ann that I think she will be an excellent big sister and that even though she might not be the youngest one in the family, she will always be my baby."

"And she will always be my best friend," said Girl #1.

Then something really nice (and surprising) happened. Girl #2 actually wiped away her tears and smiled. Girl #1 was relieved to see her friend smiling. It was the first time she had seen her smile in a long time.

Girl #1 had tons of questions she wanted to ask her friend like, "Can we babysit for the new baby together?" and "Can we teach her how to say things three times?"

But she knew she would have to wait and ask all of her questions later because (a) it might not even be a girl and (b) right at that moment, she had a party to go to backstage.

So she did what any girl in her situation would do. She looped her arm through her best friend's arm and said she wasn't going anywhere unless her best friend was coming with her.

And off they went together.

THE AFTER PARTY

"Cast and crew backstage. Time for the party to begin!"

Mrs. Denson is one person who does not need to work on projecting her voice. Anyone who is anywhere near the auditorium can hear her announcement.

I head backstage with Mary Ann. Lots of the cast and crew members are already backstage.

"I can't believe it's over," I hear April say to Pamela as she takes off her wig.

Pamela loosens the high-necked collar on her dress. "It was so much fun being in the show, even if my costume was uncomfortable."

"I can't believe how bright the lights were," a sixth-grade girl says.

"And hot!" says a second grader.

"At least they didn't melt the makeup," says Winnie.

"The makeup looked really good," I say.

Winnie, who almost never smiles, does. I can tell she's pleased with her work.

I look at Arielle and Danielle. I still can't believe they sent that email to Mary Ann. I'm going to ask them why, but not until later. For now, I just want to have fun.

Joey walks backstage with Murphy. Joey smiles when he sees me. "Mallory, you were an excellent Annie," he says.

I pat Murphy on the back. "You made an excellent Sandy," I tell him.

Then I smile at Joey. "And you were an excellent stage manager."

Joey laughs. "It wasn't always easy."

I laugh too. I know exactly which parts he thinks were hard.

Everyone is so happy and in such a good mood. Even though being in the show was lots of fun, I can already tell that being at the after party will be even better.

I can't believe how much is going on backstage. Near the cast and crew, there's a big table set up with cookies and chips and drinks. There are also a lot of parents walking around, including mine. When Mom and Dad see me, they give me a big hug. "Mallory, we're so proud of you," says Dad.

"Should we call you Annie, or should we call you Mallory?" Mom asks with a smile. Then she squeezes my shoulders. "Sweetheart, you did a wonderful job."

"You're not the only one who thinks she did a wonderful job," says an unfamiliar voice behind me. I turn around to see who is doing the talking. It's a man I've never seen before.

"Hello, Mallory," says the man. "My name is Oliver Rose, and I'm with *The Fern Falls Reporter*. We're running a story about tonight's performance in tomorrow's paper, and I'd like to ask you a few questions."

Wow! I can't believe it! "I'm going to be in the newspaper?" I ask Mr. Rose.

He smiles and nods. Then he gets out a notebook. He starts asking me questions.

Did I enjoy being onstage? Was I pleased with the performance I gave as the lead? Am I planning to do more shows in the future?

Mr. Rose writes in his notebook while I answer his questions. He takes my picture.

"You sounded like a real movie star," Mary Ann whispers in my ear.

I giggle and do a movie star pose. "I hope I looked like one."

Mary Ann laughs. Then we walk over to the snack table. All this acting and answering questions has made me hungry. I reach for a handful of cookies.

But the cookies never make it from my hand to my mouth.

Mrs. Denson stands on a chair. "Attention, everyone," she says. "I have a few things I'd like to say."

Everyone gathers around Mrs. Denson.

"I want to congratulate all of you on a

job well done. This is the first time we've done a play at the elementary school, and it won't be the last. You were all a fine bunch of actors and an outstanding crew. You could give my middle school students a run for their money any day."

When Mrs. Denson says that, everyone claps and cheers.

Mrs. Denson smiles and waits for the noise to die down. When it finally does, she continues. "Without each and every one of you, this show would not have been possible. Whether you played a big role, a small role, or you were part of the crew, each and every one of you made tonight the tremendous success that it was."

She pauses like she's done. Then she keeps talking. "I also want to give special recognition to our star, Mallory McDonald." She motions for me like she wants me to come to the front of the crowd where she is standing. When I do, Mrs. Denson gets down off her chair. She hands me a big bunch of carnations.

"The star always gets flowers," she says.

I thank Mrs. Denson. Then I look at Mom. She hands me a large bunch of roses that she bought at the grocery store this afternoon.

"And so does the director!" I give Mrs. Denson the roses. "These are from everyone," I tell her. "Thanks for being an awesome director."

"Three cheers for the director!" says Joey.

There are lots of *hip, hip, hoorays.*

Mrs. Denson thanks everyone. "Enough speeches. Time to party. Eat, drink, and as they say in the theater world, be merry!"

Noise fills up the area backstage. I watch as everyone eats cookies and chips and talks and laughs. Mary Ann comes over to where I'm standing. "It's so cool that you got flowers," she says.

I look down at them. I think it is even cooler that my best friend is back to being my best friend.

I look around backstage. Kids are starting to change out of their costumes. It is beginning to look more like the regular world of Fern Falls and less like Annie's world.

Mrs. Denson put her arm around me. "Mallory, sometimes actors experience a letdown when the show is over and the theater goes dark. They've spent so much time working on the show that often it is hard for them to leave the drama behind and go back to life as usual." She gives me a serious look. "Do you think you will be OK?"

I don't even have to think about Mrs. Denson's question. "I've had enough drama in my life to last for a long time," I tell her.

Mrs. Denson nods like she understands. "That's fine. But I hope you will be up for a little more drama when you get to middle school."

I shake my head. "Mrs. Denson, I'm only in fourth grade. I won't be in middle school for a long time."

Mrs. Denson smiles. "You'll be there before you know it, and when you arrive, I sincerely hope you will try out for the middle school play."

Now it's my turn to smile. "Being in a middle school play sounds like a lot of fun."

"I'm glad you think so," says Mrs. Denson.

Mom and Dad walk over to where I'm standing. "You must be exhausted," says Mom.

"Can we take our star home?" asks Dad.

I nod. "Tonight this was a magical place. Tomorrow, it will be a plain old auditorium," I say.

Dad laughs. "Sweet Potato, that sounds very dramatic."

As we leave, I look at the stage one last time. I hope that's the last bit of drama in my life for a long time.

TAKING CARE OF BUSINESS

As I leave the auditorium with Mom and Dad, I see someone else leaving at the same time. Actually, I see two someone elses, and they're just the people I want to talk to.

"Can you give me just a minute?" I ask my parents. "I have some business I need to take care of."

Mom and Dad tell me they will wait for me in the car.

I walk over to Arielle and Danielle and stand in front of them as they walk out the door. Even though they could walk around me, they stop like they know I'm blocking their path.

"Mallory, great job tonight," says Arielle.

"Really great," says Danielle.

Right now, compliments are not what I want to hear from them. "Why did you send the email that I wrote to you to Mary Ann?" Even though I'm mad, I try to keep my voice calm.

Arielle looks at Danielle like she should be the one to answer. Danielle gives Arielle the same look back.

Neither one of them say a thing.

I put my hands on my hips and tap my foot like I don't want to be kept waiting for an answer for much longer. I ask my question again, but this time, it doesn't come out so calmly.

"Mallory, you don't have to get so upset," says Arielle.

"Yeah," says Danielle. "The show is over. You don't have to be so dramatic."

I ask my question again. This time it sounds even less calm.

Arielle shakes her head like she can't understand the way I'm acting. "We both just told you what a great job you did tonight. We were trying to be nice."

She looks at Danielle. "Right?"

Danielle nods like she agrees with Arielle.

I can see this isn't going to be easy. I try to explain things in a way they will understand. "I sent you the email last night because I thought we were friends. I don't understand why you would send it to Mary Ann. I shouldn't have written it. But you shouldn't have sent it to her. It hurt her feelings."

Arielle rolls her eyes like I'm being silly. "It was no big deal," she says.

"Yeah," says Danielle. "And it's late, and we're supposed to be home by now." She links her arm through Arielle's like they have to leave and the conversation is over.

I try to think of what I want to say next. Then I think about what Joey said about not trusting them and about them not being my friends. He was right.

The truth is, if Arielle and Danielle could do what they did, they are not my friends, and it doesn't really matter what I say to them. Even though we were in the same cast, and for a while, it felt like we were friends or family or whatever you want to call it, I know it wasn't real.

I step aside and watch as they walk arm and arm down the sidewalk.

I have never been more sure about who my real friends are.

A SURPRISE
ENDING

Knock. Knock. Knock.

Someone is knocking on my window. I roll over in bed and look at the clock on my nightstand table. 7:32 a.m. At this hour, there is only one someone it can be . . . Mary Ann.

I don't know if it was the play or the after party, but I feel like I could stay in bed all day. I roll back over.

Knock. Knock. Knock.

Staying in bed all day is definitely NOT an option. I get up and open my curtains. "Password, please," I mouth through the glass.

When I open my window, four things come tumbling through it: Mary Ann, her pillow, a blanket, and a huge shopping bag. "We're going to have a post-performance sleepover!" she says with a smile.

I rub the sleepies out of my eyes. "How can we have a sleepover if it's already morning?"

Mary Ann laughs like what I said was funny, even though I didn't mean for it to be.

Then she sets up her pillow and blanket on my floor and pats the blanket like she wants me to sit down too. "We're not actually going to do much sleeping," she says.

I smile my first smile of the day. Mary Ann is definitely herself again.

When I'm seated, she opens up her shopping bag. "I have some surprises for you."

All of a sudden, I feel awake and guilty. "But I don't have any surprises for you," I say to Mary Ann.

Mary Ann laughs. "You can give me surprises another day. I just hope you like what I brought."

Something tells me I'm going to love it.

I watch as Mary Ann sticks her hand in the bag and pulls out a newspaper.

My smile turns to a frown. Mom and Dad and sometimes even Max like to read the morning paper, but I'm not much of a fan.

"What's so exciting about a newspaper?" I ask Mary Ann.

She doesn't say a thing as she opens the paper and spreads it out in front of me. "Look!" she says like she's a teacher, I'm her student, and she's showing me something important in a textbook.

When I look at what she's pointing to, I can hardly believe what I'm seeing.

There's an article in the Fern Falls newspaper about last night's performance, and my name and my picture are in it!

"I've never been so excited to read a newspaper."

Mary Ann looks over my shoulder as I read out loud. There's even a quote by me.

"Wow!" I say when I'm done reading. "I can't believe I was actually in the newspaper."

Mary Ann takes a pair of scissors out of her shopping bag and starts cutting the article out of the newspaper.

"Hold this," she says when she's done cutting.

I don't know what Mary Ann is up to, but I know it's something. I hold onto the article while she pulls something else out of her shopping bag.

"This is for you," she says.

I put down the article and unwrap a package covered in tissue paper. When I'm done, I can't believe what I'm seeing. It's a scrapbook, and from looking at the cover, it's from last night's show. I open the book and start turning the pages.

It's amazing. There are pictures in it from the play last night. "I love it," I tell Mary Ann. "But I don't understand. How could you make this so fast?"

Mary Ann laughs. "A little birdie helped me."

I think for a minute. "Is the little birdie more like a big birdie and you call her Mom?"

Mary Ann nods her head yes. "Mom printed out the pictures, and I glued them in."

I close the book. "Thanks so much," I tell Mary Ann. "I really love it."

Mary Ann smiles like she's glad that I do.

I take a deep breath. "I have something for you too," I tell my best friend.

She looks confused. "I thought you said you didn't have anything for me."

"I don't actually have anything to give you, but I have something I want to tell you," I say to Mary Ann.

Before she has a chance to say anything, I keep talking.

"I'm really, really, really sorry I wasn't a good friend to you during the last few weeks. I should have known there was a reason that you weren't talking to me. I should have tried to talk to you and find out what was wrong." I rub the fur on Cheeseburger's back. "I was so busy thinking about what was going on in my life that I didn't think that there might be something big going on in yours."

Mary Ann shakes her head like it wasn't all my fault. "I'm really sorry too. I know being in the play was a big deal, and I should have been there for you." She pauses and then keeps talking. "I've always told you everything. I should have told you this too."

She wipes her eyes like she's going to cry. "It was just really hard for me to think about you being in a play. All I could think about is that my mom is going to have a baby."

I put my arm around Mary Ann. "It will be OK," I tell her. "We can babysit together and teach the baby how to say things three times."

"Do you think we can paint her toenails when she's a baby?" asks Mary Ann.

"What if it's a boy?" I say.

Mary Ann bursts out laughing. "We can paint his toenails too."

I laugh with Mary Ann. "It really will be OK. And if it's not, you have to promise to always tell me what's wrong."

Mary Ann gets a serious look on her face. "Let's promise to always tell each other everything."

I hold my pinkie up in the air. "Pinkie swear?"

Mary Ann wraps her pinkie around mine, and we pinkie swear.

Mary Ann gasps. "I can't believe it. There's something else I forgot to tell you."

I can't believe there's something else. "Between the play and last night, don't you think we've had enough drama?" I ask Mary Ann.

She laughs. "What I have to tell you isn't dramatic at all." She reaches into her bag and pulls out another box. "We're having breakfast in bed!"

I like that idea. I take a doughnut out of the box and take a bite.

Mary Ann puts the box on the blanket.

"I have one more teeny, tiny surprise."

We've talked. I've opened my presents. Mary Ann and I pinkie swore. I can't imagine what else she has. But I don't have to imagine for long.

Mary Ann takes a glue stick out of the bag and opens up the scrapbook that she made. "We just need to glue the article from the paper in here."

When she's done, she takes a bite of a doughnut, and then she puts it down. "Let's make another pinkie swear that we'll always be best friends."

I shake my head. "I can't make a pinkie swear that we'll always be best friends," I tell her.

Mary Ann looks confused, so I un-confuse her. "I can't make a pinkie swear that we'll always be best friends because we *will* always be best, best, best friends."

We clink our doughnuts together like we're grown-ups making a toast with champagne glasses. Even though being the star in a play was a lot of fun, it isn't nearly as much fun as having a sleepover, especially one where there's no sleeping, with my best, best, best friend.

PHOTOS AND REVIEWS

I love, love, love the scrapbook that Mary Ann made for me.

It has the review from the newspaper.

THE FERN FALLS REPORTER

Though it got off to a slow start, the students of Fern Falls Elementary put on a wonderful performance of *Annie* last night. It was standing room only in the school auditorium last night as Miss Mallory McDonald, playing the role of Annie, led her schoolmates in a flawless performance. Miss McDonald said she enjoyed the acting experience very much. "It's fun being someone else for a while, but it's always nice to get back to your

own life." Miss McDonald's friends and family all say that they were very proud of her performance.

Mary Ann also put in lots of great photos from the night. I love the one of me with the cast after the show.

I also like
the one of
me singing.

But my favorite one is of me with Mary Ann after the show.

As happy as I was to have the lead in the play and read the great review in the paper, nothing makes me as happy as knowing that I have a best friend like Mary Ann.

A RECIPE

Nothing is more fun than going to the theater to see a play or musical, but watching one at home can be fun too. Here's a recipe to make sure you have a great time!

INGREDIENTS:
One play or musical
Lots of delicious snacks
Plenty of friends

STEP 1: Go to the nearest video store and look in the section with plays and musicals. Rent something that looks good. Better yet, rent several that look good.

STEP 2: Get busy making snacks. You will need lots of yummy things to eat while you are watching. My favorites are popcorn and lemonade.

STEP 3: Call your friends and invite them over to watch with you.

(Even though it's really fun being in a play, it's just as much fun watching them with your friends.)

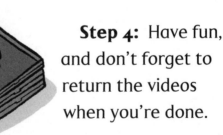

Step 4: Have fun, and don't forget to return the videos when you're done.

I hope you have just as much fun with plays as I did!
Big, huge hugs and kisses!
Mallory

Darby Creek
A division of Lerner Publishing Group, Inc.
241 First Avenue North
Minneapolis, MN 55401 U.S.A.

Website address: www.lernerbooks.com

Library of Congress Cataloging-in-Publication Data

Friedman, Laurie B.
    #14 Mallory in the spotlight / by Laurie Friedman ; illustrations by
Jennifer Kalis.
      p.   cm.
    Summary: When Mallory gets the lead in the school play, she cannot
understand why her best friend Mary Ann is not just as excited as she is,
but eventually she finds out—and learns who her real friends are.
    ISBN: 978-0-8225-8884-9 (trade hard cover : alk. paper)
    [1. Theater—Fiction. 2. Secrets—Fiction. 3. Friendship—Fiction. 4. Schools—
Fiction.] I. Kalis, Jennifer, ill. II. Title.
PZ7.F89773Mah 2010
[Fic]—dc22
                                                                    2009045341

Manufactured in the United States of America
2 — BP — 1/15/11

FSC
www.fsc.org
MIX
Packaging from
responsible sources
FSC® C008955